GRANDPA'S CARDIGAN

by Joy Watson

Illustrated by Wendy Hodder

READ BY READING

Ashton Scholastic

Auckland Sydney New York Toronto London

Grandma looked at Grandpa's old grey cardigan.
"You need a new cardigan," she said.

"Why?" said Grandpa.
"What's wrong with this one?"

Grandma sighed.
"It has holes in the pockets," she said.
"The seams have come apart under the arms,
and three of the buttons are missing."

"But it's so comfortable," Grandpa told her.
"I wear it every day."

"I know you do," said Grandma, frowning.
"And it looks like it!"

Grandpa looked in the mirror.
He sighed. His cardigan did look very shabby.
"You know something? I think you're right.
I do need a new cardigan."

"What did you say?" gasped Grandma.

"I said you're right," said Grandpa.
"I'll buy a new cardigan tomorrow."

Grandma was surprised,
but she quickly took the old cardigan away
before Grandpa changed his mind.

She darned the holes in the pockets.
She mended the seams under the arms.
She sewed on three buttons,
and she washed and pressed it.

Then she put it out for a used clothing collection.
"There!" she said, rubbing her hands together.
"That's the last we'll see of that old thing."

The next day, Grandpa caught the bus into town.
He entered a big department store
and made his way to the menswear department.

A young man came up to him.
"Hello," said Grandpa.
"I'm looking for a comfortable,
grey woollen cardigan
that's not too expensive, please."

9

"Oh dear," said the young man.
"We've got plenty of greens and blues,
and a very nice style in brown, but...
does it have to be grey?"

"Yes it does. I like grey," Grandpa replied.
"Well, I'm sorry sir," said the young man.
"We have no grey cardigans at all.
I'm afraid we can't help you."

Grandpa left the department store
and went over the street to a menswear shop.

"Hello," Grandpa said to the saleswoman inside,
"I'm looking for a comfortable, grey woollen cardigan
that's not too expensive, please."

"Certainly, sir," said the woman,
and she hurried away to the back of the shop.
She soon returned with a grey woollen cardigan
over her arm.
"Here, try this on, sir," she told Grandpa.

Grandpa took off his jacket
and pulled on the cardigan.
"This cardigan is very tight under the arms,
and the wool is very prickly," Grandpa complained.

"It's the only grey wool cardigan we have left,
I'm afraid, sir," said the saleswoman.

"No, I'm sorry, but it won't do,"
said Grandpa, taking off the cardigan.
"I'm looking for a comfortable cardigan."

Further up the road was another menswear shop.
In went Grandpa.

"Hello," he said to the man behind the counter.
"I'm looking for a comfortable, grey woollen cardigan
that's not too expensive, please."

The man looked at him and took out a tape measure.
"You'll need a Large," he said.
"Now, let me see ... here's a nice one in lambswool.
Feel how soft that is.
And this one has a lovely cable up the front.
Very smart! Or perhaps—"

"Excuse me," interrupted Grandpa,
as he looked at the price tags,
"but have you anything less expensive?"

"Not in grey. Not in wool…
and not in your size, I'm sorry, sir."

Grandpa gulped.
"I only want a cardigan to do the gardening in.
These are much too expensive, I'm afraid."

The salesman smiled.
"I suppose they *are* a bit expensive
for wearing in the garden," he said.

Grandpa thanked him and went out.

He tried a couple more shops,
but nowhere could he find
what he was looking for.
"I might as well go home," he thought, tiredly.

On the way to the bus stop
he walked down a side street
and saw a sign that read 'Opportunity Shop'.

"I'll try this one last shop," he said to himself.
He pushed open the door
and a bell tinkled as he walked inside.
There was a chair beside the counter
and he sat down thankfully.
His feet were so sore!

After a moment, a shop assistant came out.
"Just resting, are you?" she asked cheerily.
"Or can I help you find something?"

Grandpa shook his head.
"Somehow, I doubt it," he said sadly.
"Nobody seems to sell what I want.
I'm looking for a comfortable, grey woollen cardigan
that's not too expensive."

The young woman smiled.
"Well now, you might just be lucky!
A cardigan like that came in just this morning.
I'll see if it's still here."

She bustled over to the 'New Arrivals' rack
and found the cardigan.
"Here it is! Would you like to try it on?"

Grandpa took off his jacket.
Then he put on the cardigan
the young woman handed to him.

It was a comfortable, grey woollen cardigan.
There were no holes in the pockets.
The seams were neatly stitched
and it had all its six buttons.
Even the price was just right.

Grandpa beamed. "I'll take it!" he said.
"It's just what I've been looking for."

The young woman put the cardigan in a bag.
"It looks as though it was made for you," she said.

Grandpa chuckled as he took his parcel
and hurried to the bus stop.
He didn't even feel tired any more!

"Well, did you buy a new cardigan?"
asked Grandma when he arrived home.

"Yes, I did — a real beauty!" Grandpa replied.
"It's just like my old one."

He proudly took the cardigan out of the bag.

Grandma could hardly believe her eyes.
She was looking at Grandpa's old grey cardigan!

And she was so surprised
that she didn't say a single word.